FAST & FURIOUS
SPY RACERS
THE STOLEN VAULT

by Landry Q. Walker
Illustrated by
Patrick Spaziante

PENGUIN YOUNG READERS LICENSES
An Imprint of Penguin Random House LLC, New York

Photo credit: cover (texture on title) Sakkmesterke/iStock/Getty Images Plus

Published by Penguin Young Readers Licenses, an imprint of
Penguin Random House LLC, New York. Printed in the USA.

Visit us online at www.penguinrandomhouse.com.

ISBN 9780593094976   10 9 8 7 6 5 4 3 2 1

CHAPTER 1

"Outta the way, slowpoke!" Tony Toretto yelled into the comm system of his sleek race car. With a wide grin, he pushed down on the gas pedal, swerving past the heavy, multiwheeled armored hauler that served as his team's base of operations. The same hauler that was currently cruising at a ridiculously slow 40 miles per hour up Interstate 5 in California.

"*You know we gotta go slow!*" shouted Frostee through the speaker. "*Ms. Nowhere was super clear, man! Slow wins this race!*"

Three other cars whipped around the hauler—Echo Pearl's slim, flat race car was first. Then came Cisco Renaldo's big-wheel truck, veering off the road and bouncing easily over the large rocks that littered the side of the highway. Last up was Layla Gray's white sports car, the side thrusters

1

open and ready to blast off.

"Is that the best you guys got?" Tony yelled. "Come on, we're on open road here! It's just begging us to race!"

"*Tony!*" Layla hissed through the comm. "*You know I'd leave you in the dust if I wanted to. But we have a mission!*"

Tony shook his head. "The *hauler* has to go slow." He grinned. "And the autopilot can drive it down this boring road any day of the week. No one will know if we cut loose a bit."

Echo zoomed up, slammed on her brakes, and spun backward, racing alongside Tony as she did so. "If you really do want to race, could you maybe not drive with training wheels this time? Let's do this!"

And then suddenly both their cars started slowing down.

"What?" Tony said, incredulous. He hit the gas pedal as hard as he could, but it pushed back against him and the car continued to slow. "Why?" he added, uselessly.

A holographic projection of Ms. Nowhere's face popped up over the dashboard. And she looked very displeased. *"Tony Toretto! You have strict orders to stay with the hauler! You're supposed to be running an escort mission. Save the speed for when you need it."*

The projection winked out, and the cars automatically stayed at a calm cruising speed of 40 miles per hour.

"No one will know, huh?" Layla laughed through the comm.

Tony sighed and stared out the window at the desert. It was going to be a long and very slow drive to the Bay Area.

CHAPTER 2

"You see why I came to you," Red said. "It's a big job. And I need people with skills to pull it off."

José pulled the metal door to his auto shop down and twisted the heavy locks that held it in place. He flipped the switch on the neon Open sign to OFF. It was still an hour before closing time, but it would be better if no one walked in on the business meeting that was about to occur.

Red leaned over the small kitchen table and licked his lips greedily. He was a thin man, with a close-shaved head and dark eyes, and his face was always red and angry— hence the nickname.

"You think you're gonna retire here? In El Sobrante?" he asked José and the others. "This town is dead. The people here got nothin' and won't ever be nothin'. But this job . . . I've been watching that bank for months. They're moving stuff in and out all the time. We could hit it and never have to work again!"

José glanced around at the other two in the room with him and Red. Like him, they had lived in the neighborhood their entire lives. Jonathan Chan owned the locksmith shop just down the street. And Traci Hui worked as a train operator for BART, the Bay Area Rapid Transit, basically the closest thing to a subway you'd find in Northern California.

All four also happened to be criminals. Petty theft. Small scams. But now it was time for a big score. One that would let them all retire. This would be their one big and final job.

They were going to rob a bank.

"I don't know . . . ," José replied, the hesitation in his voice clear.

Red pushed back. "You can't walk now. I mean, what you gonna do? Rat the rest of us out?"

"You know I won't," José replied quickly. "But a robbery—"

"You know I need this!" Red hissed. "*We*

need this. I got debts! We all got debts. This is easy money, and you'd be stupid to pass it up!"

"Okay," José said calmly, giving in. "Let's do it."

"Yeah, I thought so," Red said as he unrolled a map of downtown Berkeley, a larger city about ten miles south. A circle was drawn on the map. José leaned in closely, though he already knew what he was going to find.

"Let me tell you the plan," Red said, a dangerous grin on his face.

CHAPTER 3

"Hmm," Ms. Nowhere said, studying a string of numbers that scrolled across a data pad. "You managed the drive in just under twelve hours. I'm impressed."

It had been a lengthy and boring drive up from Los Angeles, and Tony was restless.

When he and his crew had signed on with Ms. Nowhere and her secret organization to work as undercover spy racers, it had been kind of a given that their missions would involve dramatic car chases and furious explosions. Instead, they had woken up this morning with instructions to drive the hauler up Interstate 5 at the most absurdly slow speed possible, just to deliver a high-tech contraption that was no larger than the engine of a car. It was grunt work that a shipping company could have done!

To make matters worse, the "bank" that the team had delivered the package to was just an empty series of fake offices above an empty fake bank with one large vault on its lowest floor. The vault was the only real thing in the building worth mentioning. Everything else was as dull as you would expect a fake bank office to be.

Looking around at her team's faces, Ms. Nowhere frowned. "No, seriously. I just love leaving LA and waiting at the other end of these missions away from my real office. Just so I can lecture you. I absolutely adore it."

"It's only three hundred miles from LA!" Tony found himself grumbling. "We should have been here in a third of that time! This— this thing—"

"A highly sensitive miniaturized transflux particle accelerator," Frostee added helpfully.

"The transflux thing didn't even show a blip of activity," Tony continued. "There was no need to go so slow!"

Ms. Nowhere raised an eyebrow. "There might have been. This 'thing' could change

the way we distribute energy across the globe. The 'thing' is worth over ten million dollars and, until the Berkeley tech team gets to work installing the new CPU they manufactured, is highly unstable at high velocities. And you all kept it safe. I'm very proud of you."

"You installed limiters on our cars," Cisco replied dryly.

"We couldn't have gone over forty miles an hour if we wanted to!" Echo added.

"Was my sarcasm unclear when I said the word *proud*? My apologies. Let me try again." Ms. Nowhere raised her hands, holding up two fingers on each for air quotes as she spoke. "I was 'proud.' There. Is that better?"

Tony shook his head stubbornly. "You should have trusted us."

Ms. Nowhere smiled as she tapped quickly on her data pad. "That's an interesting idea. Let's just see . . ." The screen of the data pad flickered rapidly. "It only took you thirteen and a half minutes driving under the established speed limit to try and have a little race?" With a flick, Ms. Nowhere deactivated the pad. "It doesn't matter that you wanted to drive fast. What matters is that I needed you to maintain a security patrol. Just because no one tried to steal this machine doesn't mean that it couldn't have happened!" Ms. Nowhere leaned close to Tony's face. "So yes, Tony. I can see that you are the very definition of patience and restraint. That was sarcasm again, by the way," she added.

"But we're racers!" Tony said, rolling his eyes. "Why get us involved if we're not going to race?"

"Not every mission involves speed!" Nowhere snapped. "There will be times when you must exercise patience, finesse, and use restraint. This trip was a good reminder of that!"

"Little late in the day for school talk, though," Echo replied.

"Come on, everyone! So it was a dull drive?" Frostee said excitedly. "We're in the Bay Area! This town is the dopest! They got everything here! I mean, Lawrence Livermore Labs is, like, right here! Silicon Valley, home of the Internet! There's so much fun we could have!"

"There's a street fair in Emeryville!" Cisco added, waving his phone around. "It's not just an art exhibit or science stuff, but they have, like, DJs and a classic car show *and* Froyo trucks!"

Layla had been mostly quiet since they'd arrived, but her deep frown quickly brought the room to silence. "The transflux particle accelerator . . . it's really going to be safe in this bank? I was reading the specs . . . and that thing could be really dangerous."

"That's no joke," Frostee added, running his fingers through his thick hair. "That thing gets disturbed, you're gonna get disruptive EMP pulses, followed by a thermonuclear meltdown. I mean, a little one, sure . . . but—"

"This bank is hardly what it seems," Ms. Nowhere replied, pressing a button on a wrist device she was wearing. A large monitor sprang to life. "The vaults below are specially designed to hold dangerous and quarantined cargo. The offices above are outfitted with surveillance equipment built by Livermore Labs. This place? It's state of the art."

Cisco yawned. Tony struggled not to follow suit.

Ms. Nowhere's frown deepened. "Don't believe me? Take a look. The system is so refined it can detect the slightest variable! Like this! This line here . . ." Ms. Nowhere trailed off, frowning even deeper. "Gary, what am I looking at?"

Gary adjusted his glasses "Ah. That's a level-five disturbance."

Ms. Nowhere glanced back at the kids. "See? A level-five disturbance. Wait—"

Gary tapped a couple of buttons. "You know that safe we just brought in?"

"Yes."

"Well," Gary said. "Looks to me like someone is stealing it."

CHAPTER 4

Deep underground, below the fake bank building, in the tunnels of Berkeley's public subway system, the crime was well underway, and José had to admit Red's plan was pretty slick.

The team used Traci's passcodes to gain access to the BART tunnels. Once they were underground, they closed off multiple sections for repair. To avoid suspicion, they wore official BART uniforms supplied, again, by Traci.

That's when José went to work. The concrete wall leading to the bank floor was sturdy and thick. But José was prepared with a jackhammer and a blowtorch, and soon the wall was ready to crumble.

The lock system on the vault was a triple-lock device that used retina and fingerprint ID, as well as a vacuum pressure seal. It

14

could be opened . . . eventually. But even an accomplished locksmith like Jonathan would need time. And that was a low commodity.

So instead, Jonathan deactivated the sensor triggers that were installed at the vault base, and José attached heavy anchoring chains to the floor bolts. The entire process was over in the blink of an eye, and judging by the lack of alarms or armed guards, they had avoided attention. But José knew that would end as soon as the next stage of the heist was initiated.

In the tunnel below, lights flashed. They were the headlights of a BART train, one that was labeled OUT OF SERVICE and being driven by Traci. But this wasn't a regular BART train. It had been modified by José to pull a train-car-length platform, perfect for hauling a stolen bank vault.

It was Red's idea. Why sit at the scene of the crime opening a vault while waiting for the police to show up? Why not just steal the entire vault and open it during the getaway?

The chains pulled taut, and with a thunderous shock the entire vault was ripped from its moorings, dropping down to the ready platform.

Everything was going according to plan.

José let out a breath he hadn't realized he'd been holding.

They were really going to get away with this.

CHAPTER 5

At the same time, Nowhere paced back and forth furiously. "That reactor is one-of-a-kind! It would take months to rebuild!" She stomped a foot, further highlighting her frustration. "They won't get away with this!"

"Hopefully not. Wait . . . look," Gary replied, tapping the monitor.

Frostee leaned in. "Man! They destabilized it. That sucker is primed to blow!"

Gary nodded. "He's right. The safe getting wrenched out of its moorings damaged the safety protocols. The accelerator is fully active now." He glanced at the monitor again. "Those guys have no idea what they just stole. They're gonna get themselves blown up!"

"We can stop them!" Tony said, jumping in front of Ms. Nowhere.

Ms. Nowhere shook her head. "Our security systems—"

"Are offline," Gary interrupted. "These guys may not know *what* they're stealing, but they're good at stealing it."

Tony couldn't wait any longer, pushing past Ms. Nowhere before she could object again. "That's it! Come on, let's go stop 'em!" he yelled, and ran out the door to the garage elevator. With a shrug, Echo and Layla followed.

"Tony!" Ms. Nowhere yelled. "I have not given you permission to engage! Your presence could make everything worse!"

Tony turned backward and waved as he ran. "It's just some bad guys trying to escape on an old train. How hard can it be?"

"Wait a minute," Frostee said, grabbing Cisco's arm. "I have an idea."

CHAPTER 6

Jonathan worked over the vault lock with practiced ease, slowly drilling through the outer layer of the lock's protective steel. Bit by bit, they were getting closer to unlocking the wealth within.

That was when José saw the headlights. Two sets of headlights coming up behind them. And they weren't from a train.

Cars. There were cars in the BART tunnel!

"Better hurry, Chan," José warned his neighbor. "Looks like Red didn't plan things tight enough after all."

CHAPTER 7

"We need to go faster!" Red yelled as he looked out the driver's-side window and saw the headlights of the pursuing cars.

Traci pulled back on the BART train's throttle. The path across the Bay was clear, but it was still a thirty-minute trip to their destination—a small access shaft for emergency evacuations in the case of a flood of the Transbay Tube.

Traci frowned. The train's speedometer was already edging past the safety margins. "Any faster and we risk—"

"What do you risk if we get caught?" Red asked. "It's too late to play it safe now!"

Traci pulled further back on the train's throttle. The vehicle shook hard, and the speedometer display changed from a pleasant green to an angry red.

"That's what I thought. We could have

done this nice and slow, but some wise guy decided to send cars down here. Cars! In a train tunnel . . ." The red-faced Red let out a slow breath and began fishing through a large duffel bag he'd brought. A moment later, he pulled out a heavy and dangerous item.

Traci's jaw dropped. "Is that . . . ?"

"You better believe it is," Red said. "Now we'll get to see how good cars drive when they got no roads."

CHAPTER 8

It was a lucky thing that Ms. Nowhere's tech guys had already removed the limiters on Tony's and Echo's cars. Otherwise there would have been no chance to catch up with these thieves. Tony pushed the gas pedal down hard. Finally, he could cut loose.

"*I can see them!*" Echo called out over her comm earpiece. "*Man, that train is seriously hauling!*"

"Might as well be sitting still," Tony replied as he swerved sharply to the right. The tunnel wasn't designed for cars *or* for speed, and was split down the middle by an electrified rail. It wouldn't hurt if a rubber wheel bumped the rail, but any metal touching that active current would risk frying the car . . . or the driver.

"Take it easy on the wheels," Layla chastised through gritted teeth as she rode along in his passenger seat. Her car wasn't ready to drive yet thanks to Ms. Nowhere's limiters, and her irritation at playing ride-along was clear. "This tunnel's gonna eat up the rubber fast if you're not careful!"

Tony swerved again, this time with a little extra *oomph* for dramatic effect. "We're racing against a train. I don't think we need to stress too much!"

And then a rocket exploded in front of his car, and everything turned to fire and smoke.

CHAPTER 9

Meanwhile, the team's hauler careened through the city streets above . . .

"Left!" Frostee shouted from the back of the hauler. "Turn left now!"

Up in the driver's cab, Cisco obliged, quickly turning the large hauler to the left down a narrow street in the suburbs of Berkeley.

"Hey, homie!" Cisco yelled back to Frostee through his comm. "You gotta give me more warning!"

It had been a calculated risk on the part of Frostee to hold Cisco back from joining the others underground, but he had a plan to remotely stop the accelerator from overloading.

From the back of the large hauler, Frostee yelled in response. "I'm rigging a remote pulse nullifier device to stop a miniature nuclear meltdown from happening on a speeding train in a reinforced tunnel thirty feet below us! And you want me to GPS you at the same time?"

"Well, I don't know this neighborhood!" Cisco countered. "And all these streets are, like, super narrow."

Frostee shook his head while trying to twist a red wire to a blue wire. Everything showered sparks, so he quickly switched to a yellow and green wire. This was a long shot, but since the accelerator was active now, it *might* be possible to send a wireless signal to the device's CPU, forcing it to slow down.

"Just keep going straight for the next mile down," Frostee said. He glanced at the screen with the map, squinting to read the street name. "What's this? Adeline Street? Go straight down Adeline! And keep the speed up. The train is just below us!"

Frostee thumbed a button on the device he was building and a little blue light popped on. "Almost got it," he whispered, hoping he was correct.

CHAPTER 10

José fell backward onto the platform as Red fired a second rocket at the oncoming cars.

"What the . . . ," he stammered in shock. "You're gonna get someone killed!"

Red whirled on him. "You think this is a game? You think we're just playing around? If we get caught, we lose everything!"

José jumped back to his feet, poking Red in the chest. "You build cell-phone towers for a living! You're not some kind of criminal mastermind!"

"I can work on cell-phone towers *and* be a criminal mastermind!" Red said, getting angrier by the minute.

An abrupt hiss interrupted the argument. Both men whirled around in time to see Jonathan pulling the vault open.

"Guys!" Jonathan yelled over the roar of the train. "Guys, it's done. Now we can grab the

28

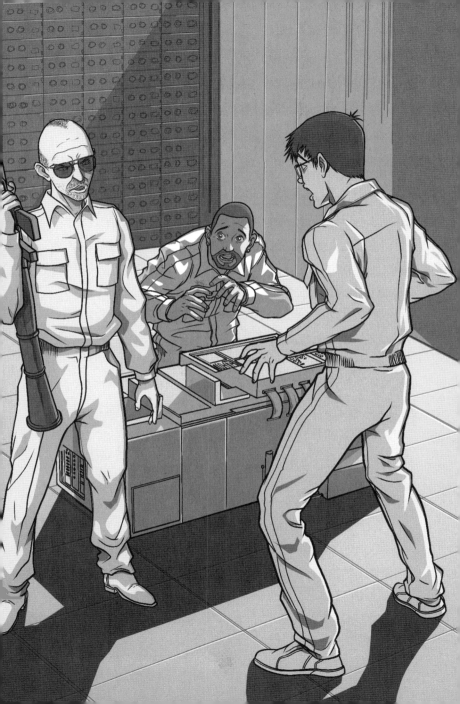

money and get off this stupid . . ." Jonathan trailed off, his voice cracking slightly as he backed away from the vault. "What? What is this?"

José and Red pushed past him to look through the open vault door. As he caught sight of the cargo they'd stolen, José felt his stomach grow cold. Instead of money, the vault contained a strange machine that was emitting a high-pitched whining noise.

José blinked, and finally spoke. "I think . . . I think it's a bomb."

CHAPTER 11

Trailing behind the speeding train, Tony, Layla, and Echo remained in pursuit. The rocket explosions had been a very near miss. "Gah!" Tony yelled in frustration. "Don't those idiots know we're trying to save them?"

Layla shook her head. "Echo . . . smoke 'em out."

"*You took the words right out of my mouth,*" Echo answered as she fired off her smoke bombs. A split second later the flatbed attached to the train was enshrouded in smoke. Behind Echo, Tony saw his opening and flicked on the night-vision mode. His windshield display suddenly showcased everything he needed to see. The bad guy with the rocket launcher was dead ahead. So close he could hear the man shout.

"You punk kids in your fancy cars think you're gonna stop us?" Tony heard the crook

31

yell. "I got this planned down to the wire! You wanna face me, get outta your car and face me!"

Tony scowled as he let go of the steering wheel. "Get this, Layla. I'm gonna drop in on our friends."

"What?" Layla said, grabbing the wheel. "That's a stupid idea. We're going too fast! We just need to take out the power—"

Tony cut her off as he climbed out of the window of his car. "I got this! Trust me!"

Layla shook her head, but zoomed forward alongside the platform. "This is a really, *really* bad idea," she muttered.

Back on the train, Jonathan and José watched Red grow increasingly erratic . . . and dangerous.

"What are we gonna do?" Jonathan shouted.

"Stop the train," José said. "You go tell Traci. She'll stop the train and I'll deal with Red. This . . . this is all too much. The heist is over!"

Jonathan turned to run the length of the

train to the driver's car. The headlights of the cars whirled and dazzled through the smoke, outlining the shape of Red as the criminal readied another rocket blast.

Not waiting to try to reason any more, José slammed into Red, knocking him to the surface of the platform. Suddenly, everything went bright and he was blinded.

Sunlight? It was sunlight. The train had come out from one of the underground tunnels and emerged into the bright, sunlit city of Oakland. Instead of being underground, they were now on a stretch of track positioned several stories above street level.

Red regained his footing too quickly, and before José could try to stop him, he fired off another blast of his rocket launcher.

Behind the speeding BART train, the missile struck, and the tracks splintered. The pursuing cars were headed right to the freshly-made gap in the rails leading to the streets below, and they were going *way* too fast to stop!

CHAPTER 12

Insistent on pulling off his big hero-style move, Tony was clinging to the hood of his speeding car, using his magnet hand gloves to stay locked in place until he was ready to make the jump over to the platform hauling the vault. Layla had almost caught up with the back of the speeding train when the tunnel gave way to the bright light of the city, blasting away the last bits of smoke.

Which was immediately replaced with a fresh burst of fire and smoke as the bad guy on the train fired another bazooka shot, rupturing the track in front of Tony's car.

Echo was luckier. She was swerving to the side to swing past Tony and Layla as the track widened. But Layla, now firmly behind the wheel of the car that Tony favored, had no room to veer.

"Hold on!" she yelled to Tony.

Clinging to the hood of the car, Tony suddenly realized what Layla was going to do.

"Oh," he said, now thinking that climbing onto the hood of a moving car that was being fired at by a bazooka while chasing a train might not have been his wisest move. "Oh no. Layla . . . wait—"

Layla didn't wait. There wasn't time to wait, really. Instead, she blasted the engine turbo, sending an explosion of supercharged speed through the pistons. The wheels responded as they were supposed to—fast. Instead of dropping through the gap in the rails, the car hit the twisted and ruined structure like a ramp, sending the car high up into the air with Tony desperately hanging on to the surface.

And at just the worst possible moment, a piece of debris struck the hood, sending a shock wave through the metal and disrupting the magnetic grip of Tony's gloves. He went flying into the air!

CHAPTER 13

Jonathan ran the length of the speeding train as fast as he possibly could. "Stop the train! The vault . . . the vault has a bomb in it."

Traci shook her head. "I've been trying to stop it for the last five minutes. I can keep the speed from getting any faster, but I can't slow us down. We're officially out of control."

At the other end of the train, Layla's car finished its jump through the air and landed on the other side of the ruined gap with a screech. The car swerved as it fishtailed, but Layla managed to manipulate the brakes to avoid speeding right back off the tracks.

"Ha!" she yelled, slapping the car horn for emphasis. "Check out those moves, Toretto!"

That was when she noticed Tony wasn't on the hood of the car anymore.

Instead he was sailing overhead.

"Whoops," said Layla.

CHAPTER 14

Tony was incredibly lucky.

Yes, he'd been hurled off a car at a high velocity while it jumped over a ruptured train track toward a speeding cargo platform.

But he still had time to stick the landing.

Tony slapped his wrist communicator, silently grateful that the unit had been outfitted with an emergency grapnel wire.

The wire launched, and the hook end lodged right into the side of the vault. The wire went taught and Tony used the extra momentum to pull himself into a shoulder roll across the platform. He tumbled over several times, crashing into the angry-looking red-faced man with the rocket launcher as he did so. The two of them tumbled together into the open vault.

Tony pulled himself up with a groan. He was very, very lucky. But that didn't stop every bone in his body from thinking otherwise.

Before he could think any further, he looked up and saw the experimental reactor that was *supposed* to be totally chill by now . . . or at least that's what he thought Frostee and Cisco had been doing while he was busy chasing bad guys through a tunnel.

"That is not chill," Tony said to himself out loud, considering the obvious fact that the reactor was glowing bright hot white and clearly getting ready to explode. "That is very much *not* chill."

And that's when the man with the red face jumped up and punched him.

CHAPTER 15

Back on the hauler, Cisco raced to keep pace with the speeding train.

"Tony," Cisco yelled through his comm. "Bro! Talk to me!"

"*I'm good!*" Tony yelled back. "*Busy trying not to get punched. Gotta go!*"

Frostee's voice shouted through the hauler's comm system. "I'm losing the signal, Cisco! You gotta get closer or that thing's gonna blow!"

Cisco shook his head. "The tunnel's gonna go underwater soon! We got a secret submarine mode on this that no one ever told me about? Because that would be really cool for many reasons!"

"There's no secret submarine mode!" Frostee shouted back.

"That's disappointing!" Cisco yelled as he drove. "It would have been very convenient

to go underwater right now! Like ridiculously convenient! Like the kind of convenient where you just discover the mode at the very last minute and it saves everything!"

"There's no secret submarine mode!"

"Dang," said Cisco, as he steered the hauler toward the Bay Bridge. The train was rushing into the underwater Transbay Tube, which would be out of reach, even from the bridge over the water.

In the back of the hauler, working furiously, Frostee began to worry. The reactor was going to fire off an energy build-up. Sort of a pulse. An electromagnetic pulse, to be specific. It was better than an outright explosion, and would help delay the inevitable kaboom, but it would disrupt any unshielded electrical devices in its range—which meant that most cars above the vault would careen out of control. Maybe right off the bridge . . .

Frostee tapped a button on his spy watch and began shouting. "Ms. Nowhere, things are getting worse."

CHAPTER 16

Ms. Nowhere cringed and considered that she might have gone into any other line of work. Anything, and it would have been more relaxing. Like maybe a job as a brain surgeon who only performs delicate operations while on a Ferris wheel.

"Electromagnetic pulse?" she yelled back at Frostee. "Can you stop it?"

Frostee's voice crackled back. "*Sure, I mean, give me a fully-stocked lab, three days, unlimited funds and NO! I can't stop it!*"

"Gary!" Ms. Nowhere snapped. "Get emergency vehicles to the bridge! Now!"

"Already en route," Gary responded. "But they're not shielded the way our custom vehicles are, so there's nothing to stop them from being affected by the pulse either. So . . ."

Ms. Nowhere leaned back and rubbed her temples. Any. Other. Job.

CHAPTER 17

On the platform trailing the BART train, Tony staggered. The red-faced criminal was on top of him before he could defend himself.

"There was supposed to be money!" Red yelled. "Who puts bombs in bank vaults? Who chases subway trains with cars? What is wrong with you?"

Tony shoved back. "What kind of incompetent thief steals a vault when they don't know what's in it? What is wrong with *you*?"

"I'm a criminal mastermind!" Red shouted in response. "I planned the heist of a century!"

"You're an idiot that's going to get everyone blown up!"

"That thing is worth money, and I'm gonna get that money and—"

Tony blinked as the criminal abruptly stopped shouting. Then the criminal fell over, unconscious. Standing behind him was a

44

larger man, clearly the guy who had knocked the shouting guy unconscious.

"I'm José," the large man said, pulling Tony up by one hand. "Sorry about Red. He thinks he's a super villain now or something. But man,

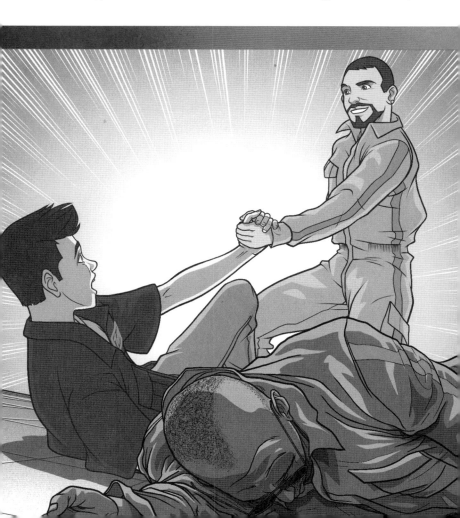

this bomb, though. We didn't know, okay? Can you help stop it?"

Tony looked at the glowing reactor. "Seriously? You just accidently stole a multimillion-dollar piece of super-high-tech equipment like that?"

José shrugged, a sheepish smile on his face. "This is our first heist. We're still working the kinks out."

The BART train sped up as the tracks descended from aboveground back toward an underground tunnel. Suddenly, everything was shadows and darkness again.

"Can you stop the thing from blowing up?" José asked.

Tony looked at the glowing reactor. "Yeah, yeah, let me just—"

The accelerator chose that exact moment to blast out an EMP pulse, which killed the electrical systems on the train's computer, but not the third rail that fed the train its power.

And so, the train started speeding up. And that in turn made the accelerator become less stable.

CHAPTER 18

THE BAY BRIDGE

The pulse wasn't stopped by the tunnel wall, or the dozens of feet of earth and concrete, or even the bay water itself.

Instead, the EMP blast killed the power of every car speeding down the narrow, four-lane Bay Bridge. While most cars lost power and slowed to a halt, some had their brakes lock up, and the vehicles slid into one another. There were several collisions, though at a quick glance Cisco could tell none of them were serious.

Luckily, only one was headed toward the edge of the bridge.

Unluckily, that one was a school bus.

A school bus filled with kids.

"Frostee!" Cisco yelled into his watch. "We got serious issues!"

In the back of the hauler, Frostee got up to answer Cisco's call, but his spy watch buzzed and Tony's voice punched through. *"Frostee!"* Tony yelled. *"I'm at the reactor and it's pulsing like crazy! What do I do?"*

CHAPTER 19

"Tony!" Layla yelled, propelling herself onto the speeding platform. "You're okay!"

Tony glanced back, surprised. He was unhooking the small reactor from its framework with the help of a larger man—one of the criminals, Layla assumed.

"How . . . ?" Tony asked her, confused. "Where's my car?"

Layla shook her head. "I used the grapple to attach it to the back of the train and now it's being towed behind us. You could have done that, too, if you had just waited half a second and listened."

"I didn't have time for that!" Tony replied, irritated. "Anyway, my way worked fine."

"You're always in too much of a hurry!" Layla countered.

The large man shook his head. "Hey, so I'm José. And we really need your help, so can

49

you maybe argue with each other later and instead stop the train? Traci said it should have stopped by now."

"It's definitely not stopped," Tony noted.

"What would we do without your powers of observation?" Layla muttered.

CHAPTER 20

Ms. Nowhere's voice crackled through the comm system of the hauler. "*Frostee, what's the status on the reactor? I need good news here.*"

In the back of the hauler, Frostee grimaced as he worked on the makeshift device he'd been using to slow the stolen accelerator's meltdown. His brow was soaked with sweat as he carefully threaded a wire through a device that was probably never going to work. "Oh, everything's just fine," he answered in a calm and soothing voice. "Why, Cisco and I were just preparing to have a lovely cup of tea."

There was a pause on the other end. Then Ms. Nowhere spoke hesitantly. "*So, you mean . . . ?*"

The device that Frostee was working on sparked and sputtered, then died in his hands. He tossed it to the ground in frustration. "It's all bad, Ms. Nowhere! Super

51

bad! I can't stop the device anymore and we can't even get in range if I could! We're on the bridge and—"

Frostee was interrupted as the hauler suddenly accelerated to a dangerous speed.

"Aagh! Cisco? Why?!"

"Hold on!" Cisco yelled back. "Gotta save a bus before it crashes off into the bay!"

"The bay . . . ," Frostee muttered. "The bay!" he then exclaimed loudly. "I know how we can stop the reactor! It's the bay!"

CHAPTER 21

Meanwhile, Echo was still driving underground, coming up with a plan of her own. It wasn't the *best* plan she'd ever had, but that train wasn't slowing down and the whole team needed her help.

Before she could second-guess herself, Echo's car accelerated. The tires shifted horizontally, allowing the car to cling to the tunnel wall. It was almost too dizzying to watch as speed and momentum carried the teardrop-shaped dragster upside down onto the roof of the tunnel.

At just the right moment, Echo reached down to her dashboard and triggered her booster rockets. The car responded like lightning, and within two seconds, it was corkscrewing back down the wall in front of the speeding train. Getting in front of the getaway vehicle was only half the equation, though.

"This really is a terrible idea," Echo said out loud to herself as she pulled her car in front of the speeding train, matching its velocity perfectly.

Using her car's ability to recharge its battery on the fly, Echo swerved over the powerful third rail. The battery of her electric vehicle surged but didn't explode, which was a very real concern. Using the additional power boost, Echo fired her rockets in reverse in an attempt to stop the train with her own car. The full weight of the train slammed into her moving vehicle. Then, without letting up on the rocket boost, she pushed down on the brake pedal.

Bit by bit, the car was slowing the train.

CHAPTER 22

THE BAY BRIDGE

Way above the bay, Cisco watched as the school bus continued to career toward the edge of the bridge.

He thought quickly. The tow grapple should work, but if he fired it too soon it would miss its target altogether, and it could

burst through the side of the bus too late, hurting someone.

He was going to have to be super, extra careful.

Five . . . four . . . three . . .

The hauler hit a pothole in the bridge and he accidentally smashed his thumb down on the dashboard. A towline sprang out from the back of the hauler, catching the bus on the bumper.

It had been the luckiest shot ever.

Quickly, Cisco spun the wheel as the bus's momentum threatened to pull the hauler off the bridge.

Frostee ran up into the driver's cabin. "Cisco! I know what to do! We gotta flood the tunnels! That's the solution!"

"Kinda busy here, bro," Cisco said, as he strained to hold the wheel in place. The hauler suddenly fishtailed and yanked the bus back from the disastrous path it was on.

They were safe:

The bus.

The kids.

The hauler.

Cisco took a deep breath.

"Great!" Frostee said. "Now all we have to worry about is a thermonuclear explosion!"

CHAPTER 23

"We're stopping!" Tony yelled. "The train is stopping!"

"But the reactor is still glowing!" Layla yelled back.

Frostee chimed in through his spy watch. *"We have a plan! Does the reactor have three green wires? Do you see those?"*

"Got 'em," Tony yelled, grabbing the wires and yanking them out.

"Whatever you do," Frostee's voice warned, *"do not disconnect those wires! As long as you leave them in, we can make this all good!"*

Layla looked at Tony.

Tony looked at Layla.

The man named José looked at both of them, then to the severed wires.

"Well, dang," Tony said.

The reactor surged again.

"I think we just lost more time," Layla observed.

Up in headquarters, Ms. Nowhere let out a massive sigh of exasperation. *"He yanked out the wires, didn't he?"*

"I know the same stuff you know," answered Gary, less than helpfully.

"All right, Tony!" Ms. Nowhere said, her voice growing stern as she leaned into her spy watch. *"Time to abort! You and your team get out of there. Grab the bad guys, too."*

CHAPTER 24

Tony was holding the wires perfectly still. There was a tiny arc of yellow energy flowing between the two. And every time he tried to move them, the reactor surged with energy.

"There's still a connection!" Tony shouted. "We can do this!"

Ms. Nowhere's voice hissed over the spy watch. "*Tony Toretto! Though I am well known to be extremely calm and mellow, I am about to lose it! You have shown nothing but impatience over and over again throughout this mission! When are you going to learn that you can't just jump at every chance! Sometimes you have to restrain yourself!*"

Frostee's voice cut in. "*Tony! That thing is a ticking bomb! The only reason it's stopped is because you have the wires set perfectly. Maybe you can keep the wires steady to get an extra ten minutes, but you can't stop it from blowing*" up if you can't move it! You've got maybe three minutes once you let go. You all need to split. Now!"

"How were you going to stop it before I pulled the wires?" Tony asked.

"*Water,*" Frostee answered. "*The fusion reaction can be deactivated if you submerge the machine. But you can't move it if the wires are pulled!*"

"We're under the bay, right?" Layla pointed out. "There's water all around us?"

"A lot of water," the woman named Traci answered. "This tunnel is heavily reinforced, though."

"But they have pumps!" Jonathan answered. "They have really big pumps to push the water out if it ever floods, like during an earthquake!"

Layla stared at him.

"I saw a special about it." Jonathan shrugged. He touched a heavy pipe near the wall. "There's one right here."

"*It's basically a two-way system,*" Gary chimed in from the comm. "*The switch is easy to reverse and pull water in, but it's not fast, and the tunnel you're in is huge.*"

"*It doesn't matter,*" Ms. Nowhere said. "*It's*

too risky! Everyone clear out of there now! Tony, let go of that thing and you can still get away!"

Frostee agreed. *"You gotta get moving!"*

"Okay, okay," Tony replied. "Ms. Nowhere and Frostee are right. Everyone's got to get moving. It's too dangerous for you all to stay." He blinked as a bead of sweat slowly trickled down his forehead. Tony still held the wires, just barely out of reach from each other. "Just turn that water on first, okay?" he said, his voice a hoarse whisper. "I'm going to sit here awhile."

CHAPTER 25

While everyone else was figuring out how to stop the accelerator from overloading, Red had been slowly coming to. The punch that had knocked him out had been a solid one. The first thing he noticed was that the train was stopped. The second thing he noticed was that everyone was just sitting around on the tunnel floor, playing with the glowing whatever-it-was that had been in the vault.

And the bazooka was still sitting right where he had dropped it.

"It was supposed to be easy cash . . . ," Red muttered to himself. "Money goes in a vault. Everyone knows that. This . . . none of this was my fault."

CHAPTER 26

Meanwhile, back on the bridge, Cisco was really starting to freak out. "We gotta get them outta there!"

"Tell that to Tony!" Frostee yelled back. "He's still holding onto the reactor wires! It's crazy! They only have three minutes once he lets go!"

"Well, do something!"

"I am! I'm telling him to drop them and run! FAST!"

Cisco shook his head. "Naw, bro," he muttered. "Tony's never gonna do that. I gotta get down there. But . . ."

Then he remembered that he had robot drones.

CHAPTER 27

Back in the tunnel, things weren't any better.

"Tony, just let go of the wires," Echo said. *"We're not leaving you behind."*

Tony shrugged her off. "Frostee. What's better? Everyone's chances of getting away while I hold this thing? Or our chances if I let it go and we all escape together?"

"There's too many variables!" Frostee yelled through his spy watch.

"What gives everyone a better chance, Frostee?" Tony pushed. "Tell us."

There was a long silence. Then finally Frostee answered. *"It'll hold longer if you keep those wires exactly where they are,"* he said, his voice cracking.

"That settles it," Tony replied. "Everyone get out of here!"

"No!" Layla shouted. "This is stupid—"

Tony cut her off. "What was stupid was me rushing off and jumping into things over and over. Just go."

"We got the water open!" José shouted. "But it's slow. Way too slow, man. This . . . this is a bad plan. You gotta leave with us!"

"I'm not going! I'm giving you your best shot. Go!" Tony yelled at everyone.

And then there was an explosion, though not the one everyone was worried about.

CHAPTER 28

Red wasn't going to wait to see what everyone was talking about. His plan had gone sideways, but he could still make his escape. All he needed was a distraction. A large one, ideally. Then he could escape, get back home, and return to the quiet life of cell-phone repair until he had time to concoct a new, even better heist.

The bazooka was a perfect opportunity, and anyone that survived the blast would be way too busy to follow him. There was a service tunnel not far away. All he had to do was reach that and no one could catch him.

And so, he quietly picked it up and carefully balanced it on his shoulder.

And then Cisco's drone flew directly at him.

"*Noooooooo! Don't!*" shouted Cisco's voice through the drone speaker as he piloted it directly into Red's line of fire, slamming into the angry-faced man.

Red stumbled, and the rocket launcher misfired. The rocket went over the heads of his target and into the tunnel wall where the water pipe had been opened. The resulting explosion was fierce, and the integrity of the wall was instantly broken. Seawater began to pour in at a fast pace.

Getting water into the tunnel was no longer a concern.

CHAPTER 29

The torrent of water slammed into the group. Everyone was knocked over.

"No!" Tony yelled as he lost his grip on the wires. "The reactor!"

Frostee's voice cut in through the spy watch. *"It's submerged! The fusion chamber is deactivated! Grab it and get out of there already!"*

"Gah!" Layla said, trying not to get swept up in the rapidly increasing current. "Echo?" she called out. "Echo, you there?"

"I'm good!" Echo called back through her spy watch. *"But if we don't roll soon, we're gonna need boats!"*

"Everyone into the car!" Tony yelled. "Go!"

As they all piled in, Red staggered up. "Don't leave me!" the would-be criminal genius whined. "I can't swim!"

"No one left behind!" Tony yelled loudly

72

amid the steady roar of water.

"Thank you!" Red muttered as he pushed toward the door. "Thank you so—"

"But you don't ride up front," Tony said, and with a quick shove, he pushed the drenched mobster into the trunk, slamming it tightly closed.

The wall started cracking further, and more water flooded into the tunnel.

Ms. Nowhere's voice shouted loudly on all the spy watches. *Get out now!* she bellowed.

With a quick burst of speed, Tony and Echo sped back the way they'd come, the water pouring after them.

CHAPTER 30

"That was incredibly unsafe!" Ms. Nowhere yelled.

"But everyone's okay . . . even the bad guys!" Tony protested. "*And* we saved the reactor!"

"And you flooded the Transbay Tube. That alone is going to cost at least two million dollars to repair!"

"But isn't the accelerator worth over ten million?" Frostee asked, raising an eyebrow. "That's what you said this morning."

"I exaggerated. It's only, I don't know, worth 9.5 million. Maybe. Anyway, that's not the point! You all could have been killed! I would have had to fill out so much paperwork!"

"What about the bad guys?" Cisco asked.

"Hmm," Ms. Nowhere replied. "Well, it turns out it was all that fellow Red's idea and he was extorting the others."

"The others helped us," Echo offered. "We couldn't have done it without them, and none of them seemed to want to hurt anyone."

Nowhere clicked her tongue thoughtfully. "A good word has already been put in for them." She then wheeled on Tony. "But you!"

"Me?" Tony asked, innocently.

"I should consider grounding you! Or wiping your memory or something . . ."

Tony shook his head. "I know. I messed up. I was impatient and I didn't listen. If we hadn't jumped off to chase them, they probably would have just been caught when they went to unload the vault."

Ms. Nowhere's expression softened. "Or they might have sped away anyway, and triggered a massive explosion that could have had gigantic consequences."

"Really?" Tony asked, confused.

"Maybe," Ms. Nowhere answered. "Just maybe. You were impulsive and reckless and you leaped into action without thinking. But . . ."

"I can't tell if you're yelling at me or not. This is very confusing," Tony muttered.

"But," Ms. Nowhere continued. "Sometimes action is needed. Sometimes you have to be willing to do whatever it takes to save the day. You were dumb, maybe. But you also showed a lot of potential."

Tony's expression changed to excitement. "Really? You think so?"

"I said so, and I refuse to repeat it!" Nowhere snapped. "Now, you've got a long drive home—and I expect you all to obey the speed limit!"

The kids all jumped up and ran for their cars. Gary looked over from his workstation.

"You think they're going to obey the speed limit?" he asked in a whisper.

"Pff," Ms. Nowhere answered with a wry smile. "The day they do that is the day we recruit new agents."